– KENNY LOGGINS –

FOOTLOOSE

WELCOME

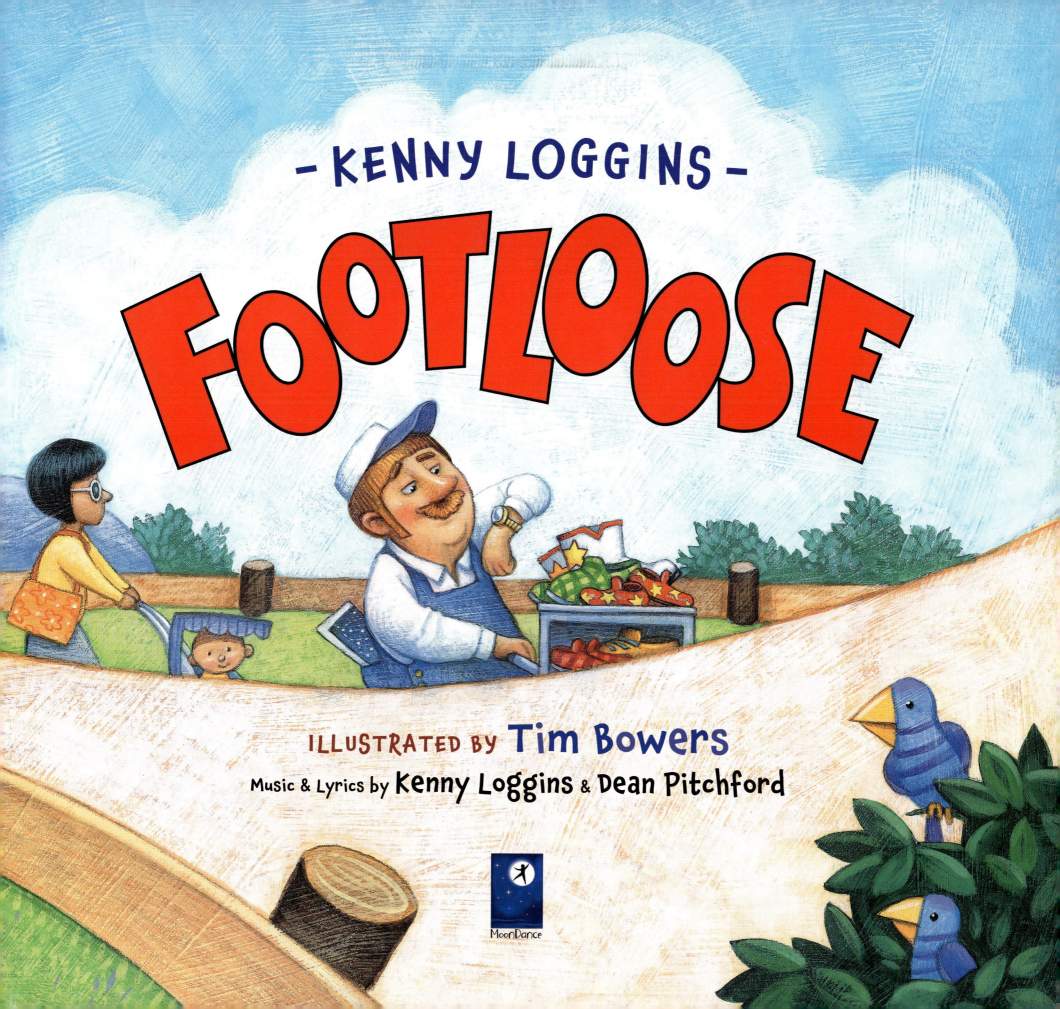

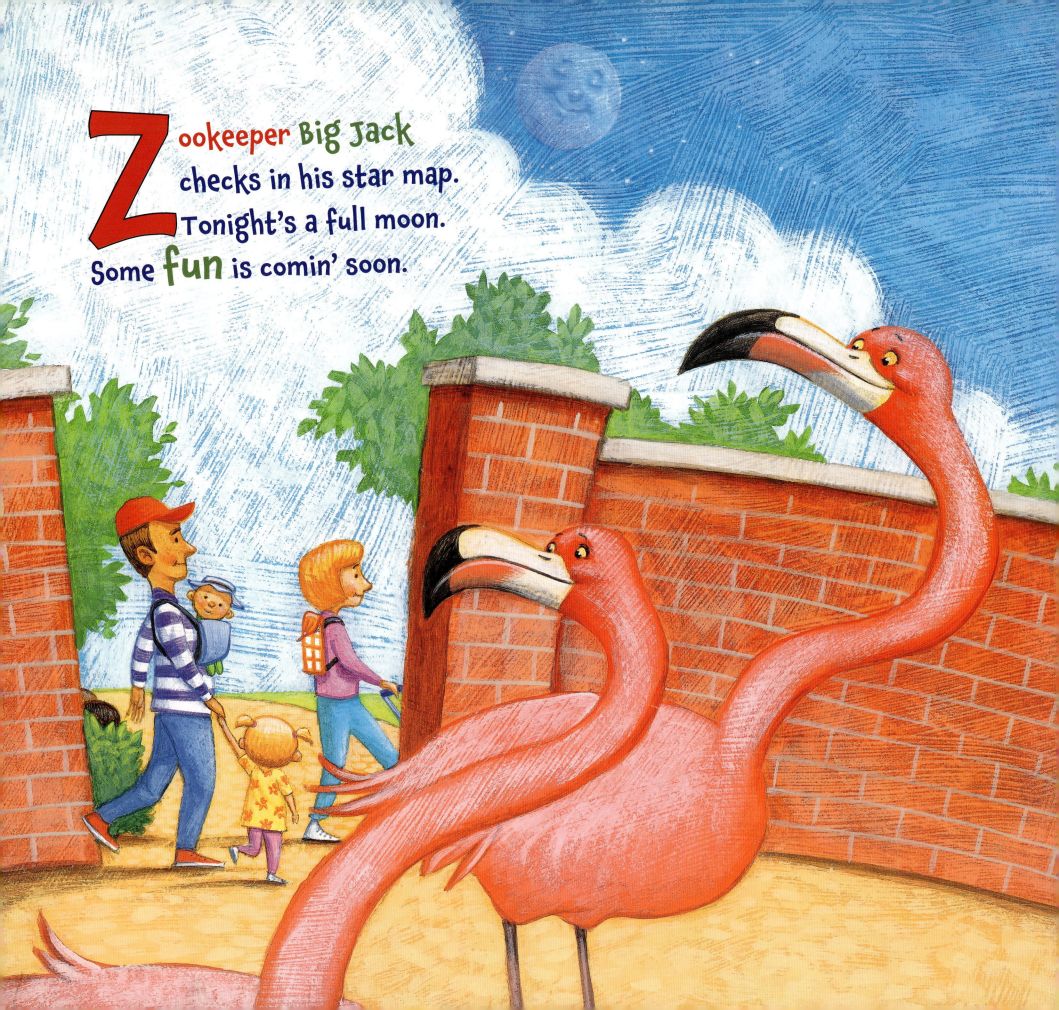

Zookeeper Big Jack
checks in his star map.
Tonight's a full moon.
Some **fun** is comin' soon.

All the **animals** are watchin'
to see if everyone's gone.
Gettin' ready to party,
they're gonna be **dancin'** till the dawn.

They're gonna cut loose.
Footloose!
Slip on their dancin' shoes.
Jeez, **Louise**,
rockin' the chimpanzees.

Jack, jump back!
Howlin' with the wolf pack.
Lose your blues.
Everybody cut Footloose!

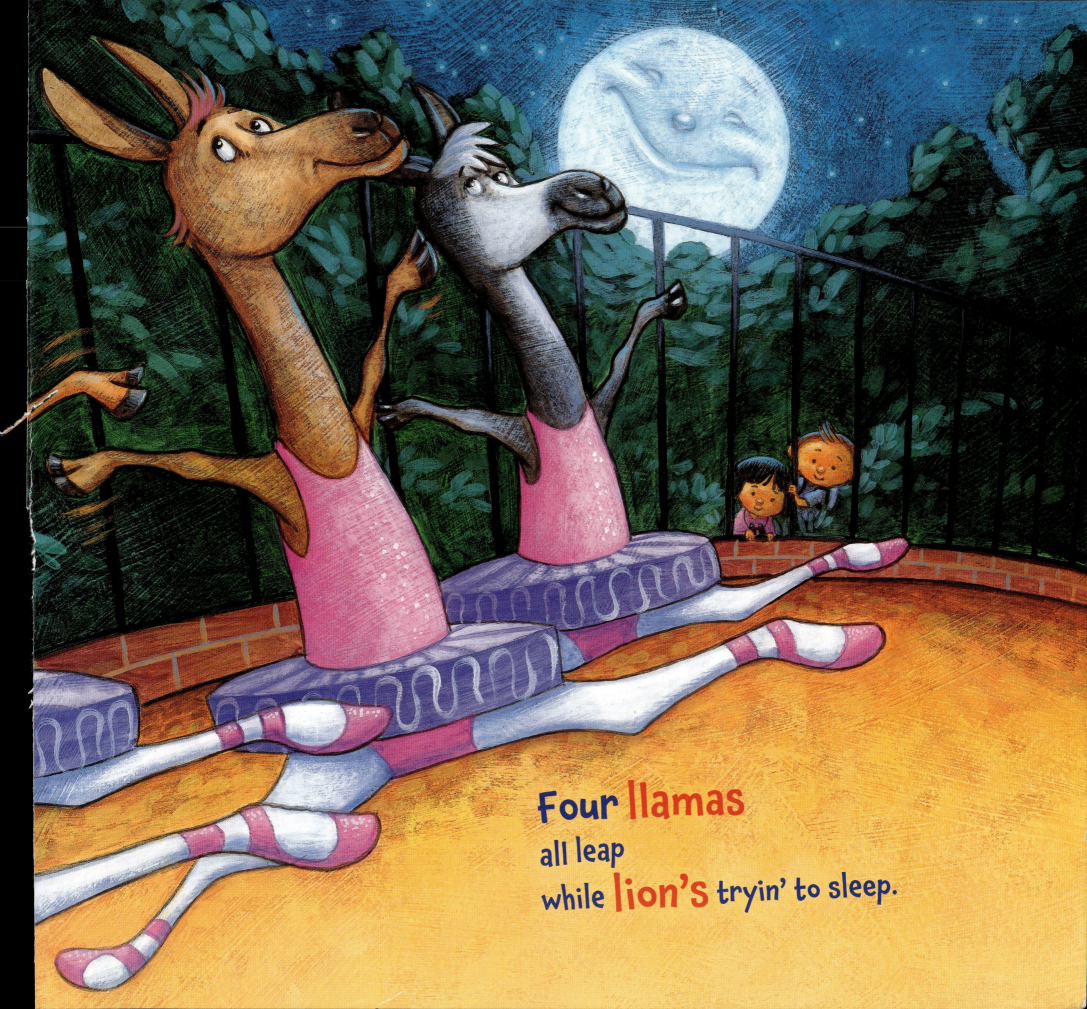

Four llamas
all leap
while **lion's** tryin' to sleep.

Five rhinos in a row,
all jumpin', bumpin' to the
Mr. DJ Elephant's
funky, hip-hoppin' grooves.
Every monkey's out dancin',
giraffes and kangaroos are, too.

All the zoo's about to cut loose!
Footloose!
Slip on their dancin' shoes.
Ooh whee, **Marie**,
who's shakin' your tree?

Whoa, Milo,
teaching 'em all to tango.
Lose your blues.
Everybody cut Footloose!

First!
You got to turn me around.
Second!
And put your feet on the ground.

Third!
Do what the animals do.
They're turnin' it loose!

Footloose!
Slip on their dancin' shoes.
Ooh, **Lulu**,
what's that wiggle you do?

Jack,
jump back!
Here come the **ducks**, "quack, quack!"
Lose your blues.
Everybody cut **Footloose!**

Footloose!
Slip on your dancin' shoes.
Ooh whee, **Lucy**,
shake it, shake it for me.

Luke,
too cute,
funkiest cat in the zoo.
Lose your blues.
Everybody cut **Footloose!**

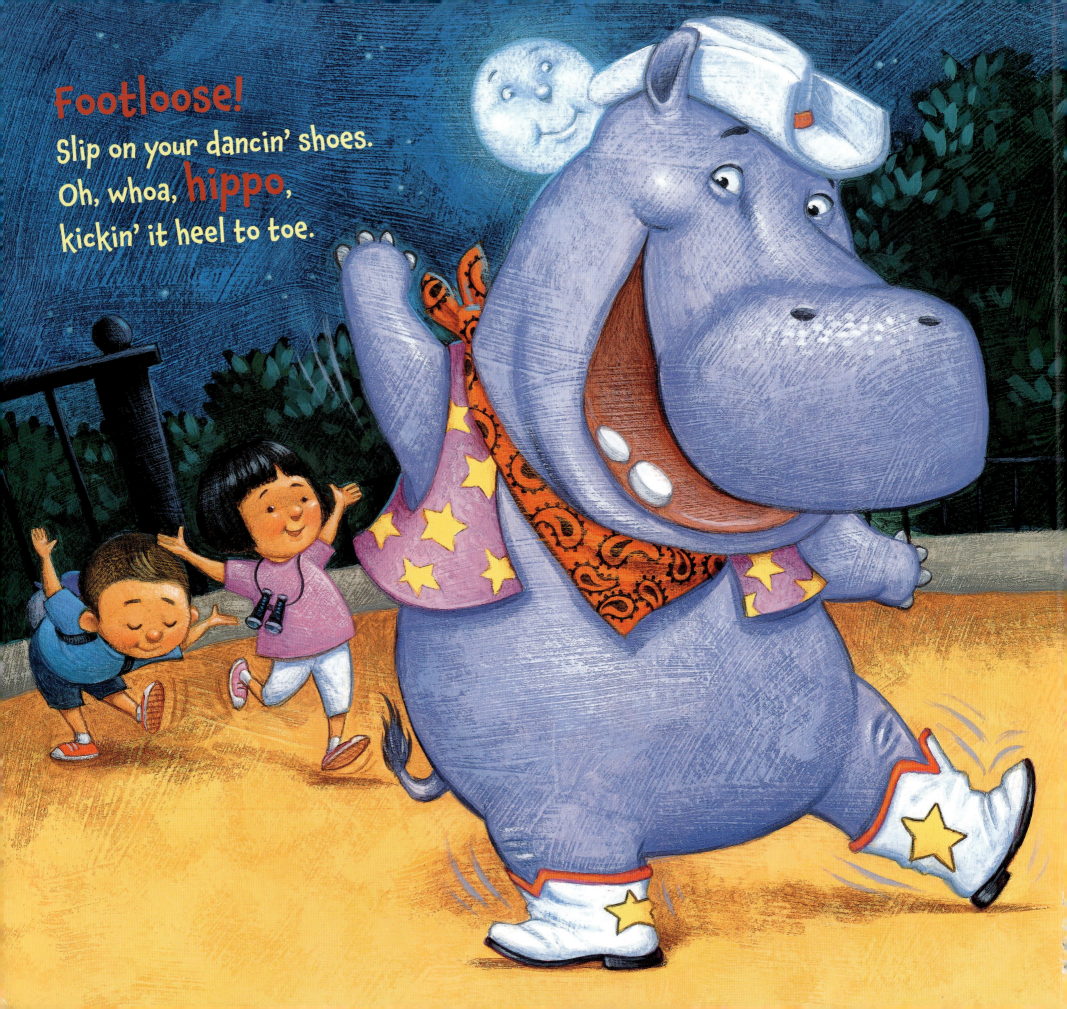

Footloose!
Slip on your dancin' shoes.
Oh, whoa, **hippo**,
kickin' it heel to toe.

Jack,
don't nap.
The sunrise will soon be back.
But the zoo's
not through...

Everybody cut, everybody cut.
Everybody cut, everybody cut.
Everybody cut, everybody cut.
Everybody,
    everybody cut Footloose!